rhyme time

Postman ™

This is part of Greendale village where Postman Pat and his friends live

If you would like the complete scene (45cm x 63cm) fully encapsulated as a playmat, together with a die-cast model of Pat's van **please send three tokens from the front covers of these books** (don't forget your name and address details) **and a cheque for £3.50 made payable to World International Limited.** Send your cheque and tokens to World International Limited, (Postman Pat offer), Deanway Technology Centre, Wilmslow Road, Handforth, Cheshire, SK9 3FB.

Published in Great Britain by World International Limited,
Deanway Technology Centre, Wilmslow Road, Handforth, Cheshire SK9 3FB
Printed in Great Britain.
ISBN 0 7498 3702 0

rhyme time
Postman Pat™
A Busy Time
for Postman Pat

Written by Brenda Apsley
Illustrated by Ray Mutimer
Series Designer Liz Auger

Pat gets up bright and early,
When the village is still in bed.

He sets off in his special van.
It's small and square –
and red!

Postman Pat does
an important job,
Delivering the mail.

He brings the post
come rain or shine;
Through snow or sleet
or hail!

There's a parcel for PC Selby,
And a letter
for Reverend Timms.

There's a magazine
for Mrs Pottage,
And a postcard for the twins.

Pat travels all over Greendale
With a card for Peter Fogg.

A new hat for Doctor Gilbertson
And a painting of Snap the dog!

"Just one thing's left,"
says Postman Pat.
"Who is it for? Let's see."

"Oh, good," Pat says.
"It's come at last.
A brand new cap – for me!"

rhyme time
Postman Pat™

Collect all six titles in the series:

and you can complete your own playmat of
Greendale village with the six pull-out sections.

Greendale Playmat

pull-out section of Greendale, Postman Pat's village, is just one
part of the full village scene where Pat lives and works.
You can complete the full picture if you collect all six
story books in this range.

You can also send for the complete scene (45cm X 63cm)
fully encapsulated, together with Postman Pat's van, if you
llect three letterbox tokens from the front covers of these books,
and send them to: Postman Pat Offer, Marketing Department,
World International Limited, Deanway Technology Centre,
Wilmslow Road, Handforth, Cheshire, SK9 3FB, together
with a cheque or postal order for £3.50 made payable
to World International Limited.

Major Forbes
Garner Hall